How Do You Take a Bath?

by
Kate McMullan

illustrated by
Sydney Hanson

Alfred A. Knopf　　New York

Cat has a rough pink tongue
to lick his smooth brown fur.

Polar bear scrubs her face
with snow. *Brrrrrrrrr!*

Elephant lifts his trunk
and gives himself a shower.

Pig wallows in the mud
hour after hour.

How do YOU take a bath?

Do you lick from
head to toe?

Do you wash your
face with snow?

Squirt some water
from your nose?

Sink in mud without
your clothes?
NO!

Turtle lets small fishies eat
algae off his shell.

Bat spits upon her thumbs
and cleans her ears quite well.

Honeybee's hairy legs
brush pollen grains away.

Chicken shimmies in the dust
each and every day.

How do YOU take a bath?

Do fish nibble on you?
YUM!

Do you spit upon
your thumb?

Are your hairy legs
your brush?

Do you thrash
about in dust?
NO!

Monkey's mama
combs his fur,
her fingers like a rake.

Dog rolls in a puddle,
then dries off
with a shake.

Duck splashes in a pond and
flaps her wings. *Quack, quack!*

Hippo's busy birdies peck
the bugs from off his back.

How do YOU take a bath?

Does your mama
comb your fur?

Do you shake off
all your dirt?

Do you splash and
flap and quack?

Do the birdies peck
your back?
NO!

Well, if you don't take
a lick bath or snow bath,
a trunk bath or mud bath,
a fish bath or spit bath,

a brush bath or dust bath,
a comb bath or shake bath,
a splash bath or peck bath,
how DO you take a bath?

Do you run water
in a tub?

Do you climb in
and scrub-a-dub?

Do you hop out of the tub?
Do you dry off, rub-a-dub?

Do you make the
towel your hat?
Do you take a bath
like THAT?

YES!

For Arthur & Lily —K.M.

To Adelynn —S.H.

THIS IS A BORZOI BOOK PUBLISHED BY ALFRED A. KNOPF

Text copyright © 2018 by Kate McMullan
Jacket art and illustrations copyright © 2018 by Sydney Hanson
All rights reserved. Published in the United States by Alfred A. Knopf, an imprint of
Random House Children's Books, a division of Penguin Random House LLC, New York.
Knopf, Borzoi Books, and the colophon are registered trademarks of Penguin Random House LLC.

Visit us on the Web! rhcbooks.com
Educators and librarians, for a variety of teaching tools, visit us at RHTeachersLibrarians.com

Library of Congress Cataloging-in-Publication is available upon request.
ISBN 978-1-5247-6517-0 (trade) — ISBN 978-1-5247-6518-7 (lib. bdg.) — ISBN 978-1-5247-6519-4 (ebook)
The illustrations in this book were created using mixed media.

MANUFACTURED IN CHINA
October 2018   10 9 8 7 6 5 4 3 2 1   First Edition